The Human Mind

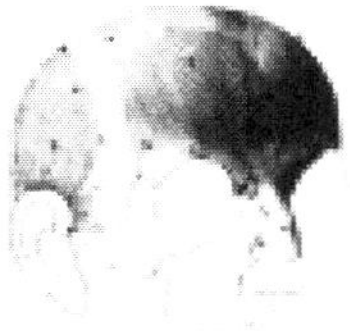

Angela Woodward

Ravenna, 2007

Acknowledgments

Several people read and responded to parts of this project early on, and others may not have seen this in manuscript but nevertheless shaped my writing with their longstanding encouragement and criticism—Cooper Renner, Mickle Maher, David Isaacson, Joan Michelson, Robert Jacobson, Lisa Black, Laura Radosh, Lee Warren, and others, many thanks.

The title piece, *The Human Mind,* previously appeared in *elimae*.

First Edition

ISBN: 978-0-9791921-6-6
LCCN: 2007936655

Published in the United States by

Ravenna Press
www.ravennapress.com

The Human Mind

The Human Mind

In 1870, the human mind was something like a rainy street, foggy, dark, a narrow cobbled passage traveled by men in long raincoats. They swept into the little stores, shaking their umbrellas and stamping their galoshes. Who knows what they bought. In upstairs rooms, women put their mending down and went to the window. Even cupping their hands to the glass and leaning their foreheads close, they couldn't see much more than the continual downpour. Sometimes the smell of liver grilling at the little corner stall rose up out of the drizzle, or a horse's whinny rang out briefly. At four o'clock, the man came to light the lamps, though really it had been dim all day, and dark for hours.

Around 1905, I went on a picnic with William James. He sent the students off to pick raspberries, while we lolled on the blanket. He described the equipment in his laboratory, "a metronome, a device for whirling a frog," and one or two other bits of apparatus. "It's so comfortable to be with you," he said. But I didn't answer. At that point, he inspired me with so much respect it felt like fear. Our hands had touched once, briefly. His fingertips were pads of perception, linked to great waves of sensation and longing. "What is this fire?" he said, but that was another time, a year later, as I was sneaking down his back steps, crying. I did not turn around, though I knew what he referred to.

It was in 1956 that the human mind became a parking lot, at that time the most beautiful of structures. Ideas slotted into neat stalls, where the sun reflected off their shiny hoods. The equality and unanimity of it was glorious, the rows and columns of vehicles, the suppleness of their curving fenders, the power promised by their long, lean hoods. Though you might suppose that every one of these machines had a driver, the drivers were never evident. They had left in the early hours to do assorted things in a nondescript building. And if on the weekends the cars were crammed together at one end while a flea market sprawled on the grounds, and if patches of oil made dark stains on the once startlingly even surface, and if the little trees planted for shade failed to grow but stood stunted and sunburnt inside their wire cages, this was not part of the official version.

And once—but when was this?—the human mind was a moth, a luminous night insect, clinging to the trunk of an enormous tree. The forest hummed with the howl of wolves, even of werewolves. Snakes and rodents rustled the underbrush. Beetles, fungus and bacteria picked apart corpses and reduced logs to dank powder. Through a gap where lightning had burnt the top off an oak, a frightening glow poured off that strange disk in the sky. The moth's wings flapped and it flew waveringly upward, following the perfume of a night-blooming flower. Before the wind picked up, anyone who would have been around to listen would have heard the shush of its wings folding and unfolding, and perhaps laughter from the garden, wherever that was, where men and women, unobserved, lay down in the wet grass at the edge of civilization.

A Thought Experiment

Let's say that the whole world becomes suddenly limpid. Mud is no longer black or brown but clear. Likewise the snails and worms that toil within it are transparent, like glass or jelly. It is possible to see through everything. Horses on the prairie are walking assemblages of translucent struts. Wild boars hidden in the forest become visible between the trees, whose trunks flow upward like water.

Mysteries are also suddenly laid bare. The graves of lost explorers are marked on the map with an X. The vanished tribes have left accounts of their demise, and the actions of pancreatic hormones on the nervous system are now described fully and completely, absent speculation. We know who poisoned the old mogul, and behind which wall he hid the forged will. The design on Turkish carpets, which their owners once puzzled over in the firelight, are now instantly readable and plain.

Any veiled god who might have created such a world is crossed out of the equation. Lab assistants too, with their buried vanities and ambitions, are killed outright. Likewise the bitter spouse, so sunny on the surface but nursing an interior grievance—why must he spend so much time away from me, does he only love me for the children, has he forgotten that rampant happiness we prized when we first met?—she is done away with. Even the cat who vacillates at the door, rubs against the corner, then changes its mind, must be purified out of the experiment. Crooked lanes are made straight. Daylight enters gloomy fishermen's bars. Dens of thieves are now linoleumed meeting halls, ordered with rows of empty metal folding chairs.

When everything is ready, we will insert into this limpid world one simple device, a missionary. The missionary is delightfully plain, in fact a one-celled, two-dimensional creature. He carries with him a single piece of luggage, a briefcase holding his book on replication. Now he in his black hat and narrow tie goes door to door, offering his philosophy. The only words he can speak or understand are "yes" and "no." He holds out the book to everything that is clear, plain and simple, and asks "Yes?" Remember, all hesitation and ambiguity have vanished. "Yes?" he asks again. "Yes?"

Suppose you answer "Yes." The missionary opens his book and in it you read his replication formula. Now you too are a missionary, with a briefcase and a book. In this world you look like a black blot. If you and the first missionary persuade two more to accept the book, your blots join to form a block. But suppose you answer "No." Unless the missionary can persuade someone else, he dies. The world remains as before. And the missionary will die in any case, as he has cancer, which will choke him off in 29 days.

Generations must pass. The black blots grow and spread in beautiful patterns which are far from predictable. Some corners of the world remain clear as broth, while the crumpled husks of dead missionaries are the only signs that our experiment has touched this area. Other landscapes swarm with busy blackness, squares and hooks, boat-like shapes, geometrical flotillas of interaction. These squadrons of the converted sweep across the world at diagonals, then vanish out of some hole in the margins. And you who have thought all this up watch, fascinated, for years and years. You forget to eat. Even when the cancer is yours, and it attacks your spine, the interplay of blackness and clarity distracts you. When the bulging tumor forces you to hold your head at a certain angle, you crick your whole body in order to keep your gaze centered on your experiment. Perhaps it could have been even simpler, you think. The bell rings on the temple up the hill. The sound is so silvery pure, nothing could be more crystalline. But what does it mean? And then there's not even an echo left. Nothing at all.

A Daguerreotype

One evening a demon showed Edgar Allan Poe a daguerreotype of the entire universe. The demon had photographed everything at once, from dull vibrations of radio waves to donkeys dozing in coal mines. By an ingenious process he had printed it all on a plate of glass, about 12" by 14", in contrastive black on white. What at first looked to Mr. Poe like faint scratches came into focus beneath his gaze—an old woman sweeping the street, geese in flight, wood doves.

"Where am *I*?" Poe asked, and the demon rapped the glass with his claw. There indeed was a miniature Poe, lying in bed with his eyes open. His landlady appeared in the next room, dusting the lamp glass, a wondering expression on her face. She was of course disturbed at how late her lodger was sleeping. It must have been about eleven in the morning. But Poe had not been asleep. He had been too sick of his life to shake his carcass.

The demon looked like a chimp, but more compact. He stank of sulfur. His teeth showed no acquaintance with dentistry. Poe had met creatures like him before. They had driven him to drink or kept him from it, depending on the circumstances. One had squatted behind his wife Virginia's head as she lay coughing on her deathbed. Sometimes in the cemetery, one winked at him from atop her gravestone. Poe was not beyond being afraid and awed by supernatural creatures, but his long experience did come into play. "I am not interested," he said, "in your daguerreotype."

"Oh, but you are," said the demon. "Half your literary output is letters begging for money. And here you can see, not three streets away from where we are now, a valise full of cash lying open on the curb."

Poe squinted at the daguerreotype. He made out a battered satchel dumped on its side in an alley off Crain Boulevard. He thought about it for a minute, and decided that since the time the daguerreotype was taken, children or beggars would have found the money and made off with it. For an instant he thought of lotto numbers, of ciphers, of puzzles he might be able to solve with the aid of the demon's plate. But he quickly realized that he needed a record of the future in order to win at gambling, or to unlock any mystery that would tantalize his readers.

Poe had thousands of readers. He filled whole magazines with little notes, marginalia, comments on submarine life, on the wood pulp industry, exotic dyestuffs, German literature. He regularly castigated leading American poets, though he was often prevailed on to write more gently about lady writers. He stirred up feuds, threatened lawsuits, published the record of a trip to the moon as fact, and occasionally flung down one of his grotesques and arabesques, or a gentler piece about landscape gardening. Years earlier, he had translated a book on seashells and published it under a pseudonym out of a desperate need for cash. His enemies continually threw this act of plagiarism in his face. He sometimes reprinted his own poems in multiple journals, under different titles, with minuscule revisions, in order to get more income out of them. He lived entirely on what he could squeeze out of his brain, a kind of black milk of words.

When he was a little boy, his adoptive father took him to Scotland. On the ship on the way over, the captain refused to waste his fuel on fire in the galley stove, and Poe and his family were forced to eat cold, moldy bread, though his foster father was a wealthy importer. When Poe was 20 and had deserted from the army, an esteemed man-about-town invited the budding poet to dinner. Poe sent a note back saying he could not possibly come—his clothes were so worn he couldn't leave the house. The man-about-town sent him $20 by return post.

Poe settled himself at his rickety table and took up his pen. Without seeming to, he was glancing at the demon's daguerreotype and noting the ice eroding around the coast of Norway. Beyond the earth, asteroids seemed to twinkle dully. These, he thought, could be the rubble of a gigantic explosion. What if there had been one master planet, he thought, where Adam and Eve had lived? Its gigantic sphere filled all space. Anything else in the universe was taken up by God's unparticled matter, an ether of love, wisdom, and beauty. The expulsion from the Garden of Eden was really the shattering of this monstrous globe, leaving humanity to eke out residence on thousands of tiny fragmentary planets. God's devotion was now granular--floating bits in a vast soup of emptiness. It was very hard to run into any, to gather it. Poe stretched his neck to get a better glimpse of the daguerreotype, searching for inhabited places far from earth. But the demon had folded his hairy forearms across the plate, and all Poe could make out was the dark dust of the far corners.

The Soul and Motion

Believe that some things that move are animated by an interior force, a force which vanishes on death and leaves the thing inert. This means that you are taking part in an ancient story that constructs beings as containers, as if you, my love, were a cup or a bottle. And here you are walking so gracefully around the bed, both tall and stooped, transporting that animating liquid, the soul.

Yet we are confronted by other forms of motion—or are they other?—the window that slams down, the bowling ball gliding down the lane and at the last moment slewing over just enough so its fat cheek knocks the last pin. The purposefulness of spiders and crabs we can rationalize—surely they do not have souls, but they have some interior packet of need. But the motion of shadows across a wall, or when musical notes ascend a scale, or when our taste moves forward, so we are no longer captivated by zinnias, the pinks and the oranges, but sit staring at the textures of the ferns in a shady corner of our neglected estate: the estate itself has fallen into ruin, and what motion is it that has established its collapse? When our thinking itself moves on, as when we finally push past a barrier, what is it that drives, steers, or directs such a motion?

The animating force may be nothing more than a sign posted inside a hotel room door advocating egress in case of fire—here are the exits marked with crosses, the stairs a series of dark lines. Beyond, the interstate rumbles unceasing, neon glints off the empty pool. The landlord slips a note through the slot—pay by midnight. And it's a quarter 'til.

The other day I thought I saw you in Boston, standing in front of a tobacconist's, though I knew you were in Cambridge, busy in your lab. As I got closer I could see that this man looked nothing like you. He was shorter, squatter, his face looked Greek or Italian, he was wearing an ugly brown coat with a belt. What an idiot I am, I thought. But there was something—it was the way he stood, so absolutely still. That is the way you stood that day in the quadrangle, waiting for me to approach, and I hadn't seen you for weeks. On both these days, in Boston and that other day, my blood burned, and I have to say my heart leapt, though clearly it is tightly caged. But there it is, out of quiet, that interior motion.

The Man of Smoke

Clasp the man of smoke. He vanishes. You can see him sitting there, a dull gray shimmer, you can smell the wet wood, the painted timber he consumes, hear his soft crackling, the pop of sparks, the sizzle as they hit the floor. Is he still on fire? Yes, for months now. What is he thinking?

You had such an intriguing conversation with him that one evening. He told you he had wasted his father's patrimony, selling off the antique clocks, the Persian miniatures, in order to gamble at Vidak's Club. He dropped cash off the bridge and watched the fish nip at it. He is unencumbered. He looked you in the eyes quite directly, asked how you were, whether you had recovered from your illness, with such a kind inflection, and no pity.

The man of smoke's brother is made of glass. He went into the bathroom, filled the tub, and disappeared. Later he sat up, and there he was, refracted, as if he had been cut in two and stacked together crooked. It was a trick of the light. Later he drank a glass of wine. I thought he might have sucked it out of his palm, but he held the stem between his spindly fingers.

We all went for a walk through the Old Town. People stopped and stared. "It's your lovely dress," said the man of smoke. "What a vision she is," said his brother. They didn't mean it, either of them, but it was a nice thing to say.

That night alone in bed, I wondered why I couldn't hold him to me. Even if he spent the night, it was to sit in the wing chair reading a magazine. "But you would burn too, darling," he said. I could see the tendrils coiling behind his forehead, the black currents rising and turning, the flickers of red from the coals. Yes, wouldn't I, if I could?

Chance and Necessity

Think of chance and necessity as the arms of a graph governing animal action. Random, uncontrolled, unpredictable events strain against programmed reactions, migrations, economic policies—two masters sending a vector stumbling upward and forward. Imagine a rabbit foraging for greens, or a school of minnows darting into the sunny shallows. A hawk circles, the pike waits in the deeper water. Imagine a dog padding down an alley with a bloody hoof in its mouth. Always you can analyze the action in terms of the interaction of a forced program and the fluctuations of the day—the opportunity to grab the hoof off a pile of cow parts destined for the glue man's cart.

A couple walks down a bridle path. She is an orphan. Her parents and younger sister died of a fever, and she lives now by sewing hats and handbags. Her education had been thorough in the area of fancy needlework and nothing else. He is a trader on the wool exchange. He had at one time thought of marrying the younger sister. Now he fills the role of friend of the family. Everyone thought he would marry Clara, the survivor. Secretly, they are lovers, but no engagement has been announced. She suspects there never will be one. He doesn't really care for her. When they're apart, she longs for him, but when they're together, she can't stand him.

They've fallen in together in a way that isn't really suitable for either of them.

Flies buzz around the bridle path, drawn by the dung and humid shade. She has sweated through her dress. It sticks to her underarms and all across the small of her back. She is sure she looks awful. She wonders why he has brought her out here, when they could have stayed in her room. He is going on a trip, "wading around the farms," he says. He does this once a year, a business trip to investigate some of the prime wool production centers. Last year it was Scotland. This time it's Algeria. He had thought of bringing her. They would have stayed in the best hotels. But now he talks of his train schedule with no mention of her at all.

At home she has piles of felt on the work table by the window, and little containers of jet beads she has spent most of her money on. She has to work hours into the evening, to make up for the time lost this afternoon. After only a few minutes sewing under the lamp, her eyes burn. It is a common plight of seamstresses, to go blind. But if she doesn't sew, she might starve. If he doesn't want her, he should just say it, she thinks. It's no use going on this way. She plucks his hand off her arm and steps away.

A runaway horse comes thundering down the bridle path. A wasp stung it, and it threw its rider and bolted. It bears down on them, the whites of its eyes showing. The rhythm of its hooves rolls towards them, along with its rank stable smell and a rain of little clods thrown up from the clay path. The horse is almost on top of them and still they have not moved out of its way.

Imagine I had not shown you this picture. Imagine you had not wondered whether one or the other of them will be knocked down by the fleeing horse. Why are you here with me, when you might have been outside, pulling the weeds in your garden? He might pull her to the side, or she might give him a shove that saves his life. Maybe they'll both leap to the side, and watch the horse disappear around the bend. And then they'll continue to quarrel and part, and the horse is merely one more aspect of a horrible afternoon. She doesn't need him anyway. You need never have thought of all this. Why have you appeared, following my words, and how long can I keep you? The horse is still coming. And still they haven't moved.

A Short History of Zoo Elephants

London in 1826 was not too crowded and narrow to have its own menagerie, though Pidcock's was something of a stinkhole, and carriage drivers constantly complained that the roaring of lions made their horses bolt. The elephant had his own cage, though not of dimensions big enough for him to turn himself around. Every evening, the elephant's keeper took his charge for a walk along the river. The animal's immense flat feet plodded along the slippery cobblestones. Residents sometimes saw the sun setting behind the beast, his great form casting a black shadow while the veins stood out red against the translucent pink of his flapping ears.

Food for zoo elephants was constituted along scientific lines—bread, wine, and gruel in France, in Germany, large compressed biscuits of unvarying size and texture. This may have accounted for the cases of infected tusks and impacted molars that were the undoing of many captive animals.

Housing of elephants was rather fanciful—dull huts described as "rustic almshouses," Burmese, Indian, or Egyptian temples, slabs of concrete cemented together to resemble natural rock formations as they might have looked in Africa or on Saturn.

Some elephants traveled frequently, riding the rails, stopping in darling towns nestled among hills and bluffs. In Iowa, the Sells-Forepaugh pachyderms cut a path along the Mississippi. Leaves raged gold and red as the elephants snaked their trunks down to sample the strange dried twisted bean pods that fell from trees onto the hard earth at this time of year.

Even after death, elephants continued their travels. The famous Jumbo took a sea voyage from England to New York, then criss-crossed the New World. Hit by a freight train in Ontario, Jumbo's mounted skin continued to draw crowds of awed fans. The taxidermist had added a foot to his living height, but clearly his stuffed hulk would have felt no superiority as it glanced down at the worshipful throngs. The taxidermied animal felt no pain, either.

Chunee, Pidcock's London elephant, went into an enraged frenzy in the last days of his life. A rotting tusk gave him no rest, and he bellowed ceaselessly and seemed about to burst his iron cage. Pidcock called in a battalion of soldiers, who fired hundreds of musket balls at the animal without delivering a mortal wound. Finally an old sailor offered his services. He skillfully crept up on the beast's left and jabbed a harpoon into his heart. The elephant's skin had to be burnt. The musket balls had ruined it. But Chunee's skull, though dented and pockmarked from those brutal last hours, hung over the great hall of the museum of the London College of Surgeons for 120 years.

Lydia

In ancient times, only those who lived on the bayou or on the moors with those hounds of the Baskervilles knew the phenomenon —lingering light, will o' the wisp, an eerie greenish yellow, bobbing in the distance. Sailors in the tropics wondered at the glowing trails their ships left, phosphorescent algae pointing backwards in the moonlight. Deep sea divers may have seen the luminescent proboscis of certain pelagic fish, but those who went under that deep rarely survived the trip to the surface.

"I present you," said the alchemist Dr. Crafft, "with bottled starlight." He sprinkled his magic powder on the Turkish carpet and asked for the curtains to be drawn. Not only the ladies in the crowd but the men as well sighed and exclaimed as the fragments nestled in the wool began to glow and twinkle. He rubbed some powder on the back of Lady Constance's hands and blew on her skin. Her pale hands went dark, then lit up like pearls.

Dr. Crafft distilled his substance from large amounts of human urine. He believed that this base material revealed man's inherent spirituality, that even our waste was blessed. The light of phosphorous, which existed without heat or combustion, displayed the image of a soul at peace with itself, an inward philosophical fire.

Just as light is preserved in phosphorescent stone and powder, so the mind stores its pictures, reasoned Royal Curator of Experiments Robert Hooke. The brain, he said, the wonderful Elaboratory of the human body, must operate in a similar manner as the soulful substance, holding its images of childhood friends, waterfalls, or paths through forests, these lingering pictures that so animate the inner man. Whenever he closed his eyes, he saw the face of his daughter Lydia, seven years old, carried off by croup. She glowed within him, without burning, though if he gazed at her too long, his eyes began to sting. And if he was alone, he would sit down and stare unmoving at whatever hit his retina, sometimes for hours.

Disgust

One afternoon William James limped out of the lab, his head pounding, his back all kinked up one side. His hands were so stiff and knotted that he had dropped an expensive silver calibrating machine that he had hand-carried home from Germany on his last visit. It was irreplaceable, as its maker had died. James thought he might shoot himself, as his life had thus far spun out into a worthless tangle. He was too ill to marry the woman he loved, and had renounced her. He had only recently started working again, after spending many months lying on his bed hugging his knees. He had lately felt much better, but saw now that there would be no permanent progress.

He took the path down to the zoo. As he cleared the little rise at the bottom, he was hit by a pall of exotic manure—peacock and warthog dung, rhinoceros feces, steaming in the autumn sun. The sumac was ablaze, while the lawn was dry and brownish-purple, crisped after a particularly hot summer. All these sensations of sight and odor struck him simultaneously, though his mind was habituated to making distinctions, to noticing things serially or in compartments, so that the act of walking into the park was not like stumbling through a kaleidoscope. Nevertheless, William James was excruciatingly open to experience, and he saw halos, tags, and fringes draped across the landscape, nothing with clean outlines but everything spreading and trickling across categories—heat, headache, the lowing of cows across the commons, drifting, like boats unmoored, across the visual and tactile planes.

James had visited the London Zoo, where the animals had been moved at last out of the dank Tower where they had been imprisoned for almost 200 years, to be situated in brown hovels laid out along straight paths, the elephants swaying morosely against a backdrop like nothing so much as refugee cottages. He had seen as well the zoos of Germany and Switzerland, where gazelles were housed in replicas of gothic cathedrals, the foxes and baboons caged within the confines of Greek temples, and looming over these fanciful buildings was an ornate mock Moroccan mosque fingered with delicate minarets, in the yard of which two lions flopped in the dust.

He had traveled to Brazil in his twenties. One evening a bug as big as a knitting needle lit on his arm and proceeded up his sleeve towards his ear. Slugs and leeches had oozed out of the wet ground washed by the riverbank, eyeless creatures that still seemed to James to have some kind of intention, a rough decision-making process.

This day James perceived something seemingly devoid of purpose, an inanimate lump, the run-over and torn-open carcass of a dog. Perhaps a carriage had run it down, and crows had picked its stomach open. Its paws and snout were still intact, jutting up like furry compass points off a central mass of pink decay. The breeze that brought the scent of manure to James' nose must have been blowing at an angle to the carrion. The stench wasn't evident at this distance. The sun caressed the bloody mass, as it caressed the roses planted in tubs outside the zoo gates. Wild purple asters, weedy things with long, withered stems and blazing heads, filled the cracks between the potted flowers and the heavy iron zoo fence. These propagated by releasing their seeds into the wind, while the roses had been painstakingly grafted onto alien roots, so each one nursed a man-made tumor just above the soil level.

A horse whinnied, and was answered by a strange barking cry that may have been a zebra. The dog's corpse rotted and festered, invisible microbial actions tearing apart its strands of flesh. "Its disgustingness," thought James, "has the power to move me. Disgust functions physically, like gravity or magnetism." And at the sight of long white worms toiling in the corpse's interior, the philosopher dropped to his knees and vomited. Even so, he felt the sun warm the exposed back of his neck.

Habit

I sat on the gravel at the lake shore, though under the overhang of the trees it was so black that I couldn't see the water at all. This was the night it had suddenly gotten cold enough to still all the crickets. Only last week we heard them singing rhythmically all around us, but now the only sound was the water ceaselessly patting the shore. The cold came up from the earth and in from the wind, infiltrating. I understood the beating of my heart as compulsory, inescapable, and this night totally unnecessary.

It was he that thought of habit in a greater sense, not as attachment to our cigarettes but as glutinous structures that herd our perceptions into safety. We pick up a newspaper and read about a fire at a library, with no dismay at the looming woman dressed in furs and underwear splotched right next to the gray column of text, though if we were seeing the newspaper for the first time, we might wonder at the importance of these exaggerated images. Our ears yearn for the progression of the chord, and if different notes come, we are certain they are wrong. The thief looks down at the courtroom floor, while the judge stares at the tops of the lawyers' heads.

"Conceiving that the body stops at the skin is itself a habit," he said to me once, holding me to him. He meant that his mind was infinite, ranging out with its transitory pictures, "a horse's head, a coil of rope, an anchor," broadcasting across his inner vision and dispersing who knows where. But how keenly I felt that boundary, his chest against my back, his chin hollowed into my neck as his words traipsed onto the pillow—"the heartbeat," he said, "can be understood as compulsory," while a harness, a teapot, a smokestack, these are purely optional.

Symmetry

The members of the French Academy argued for weeks about the ability of the bees to conserve their wax, the hexagonal design of their honeycomb having been proved mathematically to use the minimum amount of material for the purpose. How could those little bees, with their brainless striped bodies, achieve such perfection? The intersection of the angles of each chamber was measurably precise, the physical revelation of an advanced geometrical formula. Those that had walking sticks pounded them on the floor, while the more discreet members ahemmed and coughed into their sleeves in an attempt to cool things down. The hall rang with cries of "Gentlemen! Gentlemen!"

At last the Secretaire Perpetuel stood up and declared in front of them all that the insects had without doubt derived their design from God and not from Leibnitz. This was the end of the discussion, though most of the academicians were far from convinced. They examined the busted-open shells of the bees' home, they piled up mounds of buckshot and drew the negative space between the spheres, they made bubbles of soap and glycerin and trapped the film between panes of glass.

Out in the orchard, the dark skeptic Reaumur watched the bees zip among the blossoms—could they be small machines God had set going, or had God concocted the very calculus the bees so aptly applied, and let the animals develop along this pattern?

Three girls came through the hedge, their skirts held to the side in one hand, white kerchiefs over their hair. They were laughing and calling one of them a liar. "No, no," she said. "I saw it, really. Two nights ago." They cut across the corner of the estate and vanished into the trees down by the creek. He heard them splash and shriek. A long time later, he glimpsed their white headdresses bobbing above the brambles up on the ridge. He had never seen the girls before. Now they were gone, off perhaps to the tinkers' encampment beyond the next village.

The moon rose while the sky was still blue, but presently the mathematician found himself sitting in the evening chill, a white hook beaming mysterious light on him. The buzzing in the trees had long ago stilled, and now the swallows came in silence to swoop after gnats. Reaumur sat on, until clouds covered his source of illumination. He couldn't see even his hand in front of his face. Yet he felt the night to be gigantic, endless, spread out in a huge perfect circle all around where he sat, himself the black dot at its center.

Computers

The original computers were not electronic machines but rows of college girls locked in a windowless room at Cornell, calculating trajectories of artillery shells. While their brothers and sweethearts had gone overseas, posting exhausted letters back on thin blue paper, the girls bent over desks, as they had always done, fingering their slide rules and twirling their hair. They were not allowed to tell their gruff fathers that they were compiling ballistic firing tables. When they came home, eyes red from squinting, backs aching from hours in the hard chairs, they followed a script their supervisor had drilled them on, saying they had been typing official correspondence that was of no interest to anyone.

So again we have the women enclosed, chatting or silent, indoors, under wraps, and the men on the other side of the world, firing machine guns sideways from airplanes. The firing tables the girls compiled had, on the other hand, adventurous lives. They got crumpled, torn and smudged. Sometimes the yellowed cards were splashed with blood, trampled into mud, or drowned in the uncaring ocean. The lamination flaked away in the salt water, and swordfish and petrels came to nip at the floating bits of paper.

Airmen dropped by parachute into a desolate nighttime France. The girls walked through the university demonstration garden, which had gone untended for the past two and a half years. The long grass brushed their ankles and soaked their worn-out shoes. They fell asleep in the movie theater, where they had gone after drying the dishes their mothers washed. Here, asleep, they could have rowed boats, tamed lions, or twined around handsome men they had in real life only seen from a distance once. But instead they dreamed of numbers, continued calculating, their fingers twitching, until their heads jerked back against the seat and they started awake to see an heiress running down a staircase with tiny clicking steps. Before she had reached the bottom they were asleep again, computing angles, derivatives, wind resistance, arcs of descent.

Anatolia

Robert Hooke found that in the Anatolian villages even the littlest children were given toy looms to push around the floor, and by the time the girls were six, they had authored the most remarkable rugs, cherry red grounds figured with trees and vines, cheerful, sometimes slightly crooked designs severely straightened and corrected by their black-toothed mothers. He brought back a dozen, when he had only meant to buy three or four, and still he hadn't spent all the money he had brought. These fabulous wool creations were valued like a canvas bag would be in London, like a tackle box, a saddle blanket.

His teacher, the great Wilkins, developed an artificial universal language in which he defined 40 types, and further divided the types into nine sorts, and the sorts into nine differences, so that using a minimum of discrete syllables, one could express the idea, "The white sheep grazed upon the hill." In tribute to his teacher, Hooke used the universal language to write a treatise on pocket watches, which he published in 1664.

The fire in Anatolia smelled different from English fire. At first he had thought he would be happy to get back to his familiar hearth, but once home, he longed for that more resinous scent, caused by the rosemary twigs they sprinkled through their cooking perhaps, or the more acidic sappiness of the Anatolian wood. He could scarcely recall the odor once away from it, but now his London fireplace smelled thin, lacking. Perhaps it was the lamb fat spattered against the walls of their houses, he thought.

The little girls worked into the early evening, the gang of them laughing from doorway to doorway as their hands flew over the shuttles. Occasionally their teeth flashed against the darkening sky as they leaned forward to bite off an end of thread.

Wilkins sent him a peculiar knotted string. It was a code, his mentor told him. Hooke refused to let Wilkins in the door. He had always been taciturn to all but his one good friend, yet he was afraid to let Wilkins see the jolly carpets laid out across his damp parlor. Hooke's father had been an ironmonger, while Wilkins, Newton and their ilk were men of means and always had been. They would call him a carpet seller. He couldn't bear it. How could they know what he had been in search of among the primitive weavers? Memories, he thought, were linked together in the mind, stored up like an infinite, weightless chain coiled in the center of the brain, a worm of ideas, the most recent hot and sensitive, the older memories cold, sluggish, buried under the pile of subsequent links. He wound Wilkins' string across a board of 26 squares, and found a message spelled out, each knot a letter—"Beware of the bearer, who is sent as a spy over you."

It was one of Wilkins' little jokes, but Hooke threw the string into the fire, where the ash coiled, sinuous, first red then gray, upon the slate.

A Dream

One of the Anatolian women was a witch. She had eaten a poisonous mushroom as a child, but survived, and ever after had magical powers to bind creatures to her. Hooke sat around the fire with some of the older villagers. He had taken skeins of their wool and was shaking them in front of the women's noses. "Green," he said. "These are all green, aren't they?"

The women laughed. One skein was the color of grass, one was like cedar, one was the color of an unripe apple—all the wool was different. Only the poor foreigner couldn't see that. He showed them his other hand: "Blue—all blue, aren't they?" And they laughed harder. He had water, bird wings, twilight, all completely different.

He had no wife at home. They had asked him. He had not told them about his daughter, born to a seamstress. The seamstress had made the very shirt he was wearing, and had mended his socks. Their daughter had been born in her little room behind the shop, and had died there too.

The witch tired of watching Hooke and moved on. She knit a huge invisible bag out of air and ran off into the forest with it streaming open behind her. Hooke got up, leaving the wool on a flat stone. The women remarked how thin he was, how his body bent perpetually to one side, his shoulders hunched as if he was always cold. Hooke stumbled down a little track, first taking it to be the shortcut to the upper part of the village, and soon losing himself along ruts made by deer and their predators.

"I have caught you," said the witch, opening the mouth of the bag so he could step out. She grabbed his hand. Instantly his English clothes grated up against her billowing black dress. Later Hooke woke up, but he did not open his eyes. He was in her hut. The yellow light of the witch's candle bathed his eyelids, and the world was to him an undifferentiated golden glow. As the color and warmth spread, something slunk through a door in his mind, a tail disappearing as the panel swung shut. It was an idea, perhaps a memory—the formula for the oscillation of a spring, or the shape of a vase, or someone's cheek brushing his hair. This thought, whatever it was, had once been whole and alive, and was now reduced to a whiplike hind part, a thin rind disappearing as he gained consciousness.

The witch lay with the light behind her, contemplating him openly.

The Little Theater

Come in. Sit down. It's dark. You are far from the action. There they are, your parents, lit up yellow on the stage, your father smoking his cigarette, your mother rocking the cradle with the toe of her ballet slipper. Speech has been replaced by music, the fantastic overture, promising the themes to be developed in upcoming scenes—the entrance of the sister, the villain, and finally that great good man you would lay down your life for, if only he would permit it.

On a field far off, but visible through the window, boys are running back and forth kicking a ball. From here it does not seem at all organized—the reds and purples and blacks of their sweatshirts roam in spirals. The trees are lit like torches under a ceramic November sky, the red and gold uplifted, though it's down the leaves will fall, certainly, to brown, and be torn and shredded by boot treads, and buried under snow.

The mind's little theater goes on all the time, and it can be any season—the pear trees gleaming white with flowers along the boulevard, the black September night when he took you to the graveyard, where cats peed against the crooked wooden markers. The next instant it's that party again, where just after you shed your coat, all flushed in your velvet, he appeared at your elbow, tall and looking beyond you over your head.

One day you may watch your own death play out, a wrinkled woman propped on pillows, a tube in her throat, gasping. Yet you'll still be comfortable in your seat, scrunched down, perhaps your hand in a bag of candy, waiting for the nurse to fling open the door. She has fair skin and reddish hair pulled tightly back. She glances at the chart on the end of the bed with disdain, pinches the old woman's wrist to take her pulse, then waltzes out. The doctor loves her, though he is no way as handsome as she is, and she may never notice. She has one child, but lives alone. Sparrows have built a nest in the air vent, and the outside maintenance crew will come soon to knock it down. The birds don't seem to mind the huge generator, complete with spinning turrets, humming hideously on the roof.

The World Under Water

The Greek sponge divers went down naked, the same in 1860 as in ancient times. But those who salvaged collapsed hulls from the bottom of Danish harbors were considerably better dressed. To get the heavy twill diving suit on, European divers had to soap their wrists, and their hands began to turn blue as soon as the cuffs were fastened. The lead weights hit them in the kidneys and jabbed them in the collarbone. Yet after a few trips down, they found they could move about easily.

Gentlemen visitors to London often clamored for an expedition in Professor Halley's diving bell. Young ladies went under with a candle and a volume of poetry. Miss Eliza took her kitten with, and once two couples had a game of underwater croquet within the cramped confines of the contraption. But the real natural philosophers needed no distractions. The gloom of the harbor bottom was enough to fascinate them.

When the first entrepreneurs introduced the aqualung to the fabled divers of Kalymnos, the men took to it with glee. At last able to actually breathe underwater, they went deeper and stayed down longer, resurfacing with two-thousand-year-old amphorae filled with gold coins. They spent their fortunes on ouzo and top hats. Yet by the end of the season, fully half the divers were dead of caisson sickness, the nitrogen boiling in their blood as they came up too rapidly. The widows drove out the English combine that had brought in the modern equipment, and the reduced corps returned to its old ways, plunging over the side of their queer little boats headfirst in just the skins they were born in. Only some seventy years later did the French navy compile and publish accurate charts showing the relation between time, pressure, and depth.

One of the most remarkable sights William Beebe recorded in his Bathysphere, a bronze globe that he sank to extraordinary depths off Bermuda in 1930, was a luminous fish that swam past his window. The water had been absolutely dark and dead, the sun put away, as it seemed, in a padded box, and not a ray snaked down to feed diatoms or algae. Beebe had not thought to bring a rug or cushion, and lay huddled on the hard curving floor of his machine, remarking into his relay radio as each previous record was broken. Suddenly a flash of yellowish green slid past the thick glass. Beebe began to stutter into the microphone as he described the vanishing light. The listening crowd pressed around the service desk in the lobby of the Kingston Palace Hotel could not make out what he was saying. "A fish," he said, but many thought he was choking or drowning. He was simply overcome by the beauty of the sight.

Sleep

To sleep on a train is to enjoy a constant forward striding, the brain joggling along in its bone suit, the skeleton cased in steel, the steel breathing smoke out its gigantic outer lung, the landscape ripped in two as the train dives through it, disdainful. Trees, goats, barns, slash behind you, tossed aside as you rush on, comfortable in your tiny bunk, your head on a hard, flat pillow, your feet sheathed in the warm socks you thought to pack, and all you have to do is lie still and contemplate.

To sleep coiled against him—a few afternoons were allotted to us, and on those occasions I went deeper still, still talking to him as we struggled up a hillside above a ruined city, or as he opened the door of a powerful elevator. Unconscious, he was still there, rubbing his beard against my cheek, pointing out the dipping flight of the lemon warblers that lived in the pines around his laboratory.

It was impossible to imagine that the mind would ever stop, the way it kept on manufacturing images, setting them to music, and overlaying all this with conversation, color, though once, in a dream, he was about to feed me an exotic candy he had bought at the Turkish market, a kind of cardamom fudge he called it, and I awoke with a start just before it could touch my tongue. Even three years after I last saw him, in sleep he kissed me as if we had never parted, and dropped me down to the tiled floor of the salon. This was not a memory but a continuation, seamless, his skin against my skin.

Yet one morning I arrived, my legs wobbly, my eyes gummy, mouth dry and caked at the edges. I looked around, and all the signs hanging from the vast station ceiling were in a foreign script, indecipherable. The steam from the tea carts mixed with the soot of the train yard, everything gray and mushy and covered over. But there was my suitcase, standing unattended on the platform, and I hurried to disembark. At last I was all alone, as the crowd swarmed around me, children, beggars, porters, jewelers, and their wives.

Considerations

Consider all the things that can be considered, the selenography of the moon, the weight of air, the descent of heavy bodies. We must spend time thinking up improvements to the action of waywisers (those gauges for tracking the length of carriage journeys), and record the history of royal families as well as the processes of every trade—candle-making, harness-braiding, how water is brought up from the depths of a river without mixing with water from shallower levels. Consider the orbits of comets. Wonder why a baby cries even when nothing appears to be wrong, no hunger, no pin sticking through his diaper, and mama is holding and shushing him. How are flies generated from muck? Can cotton be cultivated in a damp climate? All these things the mind can contain and explore, and the hands one day write treatises and create devices—an iron bucket with one-way flaps that spring closed when it hits the bottom, trapping the water that entered at the deepest point.

I wanted to recall what William James' thumbnail looked like, to see if from that I could recast the whole man. How did his hand grip the edge of the armchair, at what angle did he hold his head? One afternoon he told me not to work so hard as I was pushing against him—we only had a few minutes, and from where I lay I could see the key turned in the lock, promising not security but how temporary it all was. Soon one of his students would rattle the knob, or he would be overcome with a pang at the thought of his wife and children. All I could see of him then was a bit of his ear and his arm, just in front of the shelf that held his notebooks.

What to bring back from this adventure? A necklace, a seashell, a printed beach sarong with the name of the hotel—call it the Hotel Human Mind, with its fabulous bar, the old dark wood and creaking fans, the silent waiters, the fabled crab cakes. Send the bucket down and the flaps spring closed, trapping the water that entered at the deepest point. Yet to haul the heavy thing up again is so difficult, and to pour the water into beakers—most of it slopped over the side, and the backsplash of the oars contaminated the samples. What do these experiments tell us anyway? We have to know what questions to ask. James, my dear love, said that the action of the heart is compulsory. Compulsory.

The Brown Bull

It is possible to take the mind apart, to empty it for cleaning and inspection. This she did one evening while her husband was away. He went out every night, no matter the weather, and returned at dawn, bloody and exhausted. But she was not to ask him what he was up to.

First she emptied her thoughts into a bowl. Long strings and broken segments streamed out and sat in a gooey mass, slightly steaming. But soon they settled under a thick skin, like the top of a custard, and she felt wonderfully calm. The moon shone, a hook through the window. Wolves howled—the pack was hunting. No people lived anywhere near, and she had never been to the village.

Relieved of its thoughts, the mind sat, exactly as hushed and organized as a library. She prised out sections of hexagonal compartments, wood and brass cabinets slightly dusty, that held surprising things. Here were the instructions for understanding containers, motion, and the passing of time. Bits of language had coagulated, so that she found words that seemed to mean all at the same time the action of throwing dice, laying fodder in front of horses, and turning one's eyes to the side. She took out a hinged box, and inside it lay directions for contemplating the crumbling of a rock wall. Pushed behind it she found a yellowed map which outlined the separation of colors—what was blue and what was green. Here was an index showing the grouping of certain objects as tools, and a schematic for predicting the future, as when a fist is raised and you step aside.

She went over all these bits of her mind with an old piece of linen torn from the gown she was wearing when she first came to his house. She rubbed ash off the empty floor, and at last put it all back together. Nowhere had she found what she was looking for, what she had imagined would have totally filled her mind, a swollen red lump, and that was the source of her feeling for him. She knew it was near, an overpowering emotion, but it was still hidden. She slipped the cold thoughts back in her ear and went again to the window. It was so black now she couldn't see out at all. The glass, instead, showed her own face lit by the candle, floating unanchored.

Her husband returned as the sun rose, one leg ripped open, his shoulders raked with claws. As he slept, she took the key from around his neck and unlocked his armoire. In it she found the gashed and stinking skin of a bull. Did she not know that a spectral bull had been harrowing the country for the many months she had been living here? She drew the skin out and threw it into the fire. "My love, what have you done?" he cried, starting awake. "If only you had waited one more day! Now I must leave you!"

He vanished, and the house with him. She was alone in the woods. What if instead of burning it, she had wrapped the hide around herself? Why had she been so meticulous with her delicate interior? What is the mind compared to a bloody skin? To ripped muscle and thrashing bone?

Lost Languages

The linguist Malbeck hired two men to take him up the mountain to see the ruins. They were to camp out the first night, and make it over the pass to the old site by noon the second day. But Malbeck woke in his frosty tent to find his guides gone. They had taken the donkey, the food, Malbeck's Swiss mountaineering tools, his cash and his boots. Malbeck set off on the trail in his thick wool socks.

He had encountered many difficulties in his career. The unknown language he was attempting to decipher had first been found inscribed around three sides of window sashes in a caved-in guard house. It was impossible to tell which way the letters ran, up, down, left, or right. He had spoken about the problem before the Royal Asiatic Society and been told by old Duffy that the language probably ran plow-wise. That is, it was inscribed left to right on one line, right to left on the next, the writer's hand taking a turn like a weary mare. "But these are window frames," Malbeck said. "We have no tablets."

Duffy looked at Malbeck's drawings and declared that he understood the meaning instantly. It was very similar to Hittite. "I'll let you figure it out," he said, and tramped over to the plate of lemon bars on the side table.

A retired school teacher in Macedonia had told Malbeck that the strange writing was used by healers in his village on protective amulets. Malbeck then tracked down an amulet maker, who translated a stylized image of a bee as "gratitude," because "bees were very forgiving." A triangle he said meant "westerly," a slashed square was "evil," two joined figures meant "aunt and uncle." Later he said the same joined sign meant "today and tomorrow." He was obviously making it all up as he went along. Malbeck picked his hat up off the floor and walked the twelve miles back to the carriage depot that got him the thirty miles to the train station

Malbeck climbed, the sun dazzling his eyes, his feet wet and numb. Long patches of ice filled ruts along the track, and several times he had to traverse glistening meadows of frozen flowers. He was heading for a crook-shaped crag the younger of his guides had pointed his finger at. His head throbbed and his fingers had knotted up at the knuckles, red and cracked. He sat down on a boulder and filled his pipe. His tinder, his passport, his journal and ink pen had all survived the thieves, pocketed next to his heart. He had no tea and no meat, but he managed to get the pipe burning nicely. The smoke curled away behind his ear.

The sun was setting when he reached the monuments beyond the pass. Three stone tablets, cracked and leaning, jutted out of the bare rock face. Perhaps this had been a far border of a lost empire. The stick writing hopped across the tablets, more of it than the linguist had ever seen. He began to copy it into his notebook, working from left to right out of habit, though the symbols were so densely and regularly spaced that they might have been applied en bloc, the way a design is printed onto cotton. It occurred to him that the script might be entirely decorative, with no relation to speech at all. In this case, his whole project was useless. But he toiled on, his swollen fingers cramped around the pen, until the sun set.

Malbeck's rival Kirchner had knowingly mistranslated some hieroglyphics early in his career, knowing no one alive then could catch it. He had added ornate phrases like "his great and eternal all-knowing holiness" and "bringer of eternal night and darkness" to what turned out to be a mundane log of wool imports. The Asiatic Society laughed about it behind his back, but Kirchner was nevertheless Recording Secretary and editor of the biannual journal.

Malbeck sat with his knees tucked under his jacket, his hands in opposite sleeves. He could still see the ancient writing across his eyelids. It told the story of an enchanted antelope, he thought, a woman who had been captured by a witch while combing her hair by a well. The linguist had known very few women in his life, apart from his mother and sister. Once he had sat down on a sofa in the lobby of a hotel in Brno, not noticing a girl crouched at the other end, writing a letter. Her dark hair had covered most of her profile. She gave a little sniff, and he saw she was crying, her nose all red, tears blotching her cheeks. What had she been writing? 'My dearest Gabriel, how could you be so cruel? Here I am alone in Brno, while you are dancing with that hussy. You never meant to marry me. How will I survive?'

Malbeck reached inside his coat for his pipe. When he lit the tinder, a world appeared around his hand, a globe of orange, red and purple rocks, spikes of a tiny pine, a snatch of snow, and his fingertips glowing like ripe fruit. Then the wind blew the tiny flame out, and he dropped the pipe. It clattered away on the rock. In bending after it, he swept his leather journal aside. He groped in the dark, but couldn't find it. He tried to light the tinder again, but his hands were too clumsy to get the motion of the little wheel just right, and he only achieved a sputtering spark. He gave up after a long time, and tucked his hands into his sleeves again. He would find everything in the morning, if he did not freeze to death overnight. The guides had also warned him of wolves, bears, and mountain cats.

If he stayed awake, his blood would continue to circulate, and he would live. He settled his chin onto his chest, but the cold wind still caressed his jaw. His teeth were cold all the way down to the roots. But happily, the hotel had a good fire going in the gigantic lobby hearth. He looked again at the black-haired girl. To his surprise, her dress was covered with writing, a looping script that had first seemed like scallops of embroidery, but now revealed itself as connected letters. "I love Johannes Malbeck," the fabric proclaimed. He looked at her, astonished, and she gazed right back at him, her face still mournful and stained. "My dear," he said, and put out his hand. In an instant she was wrapped around him, her hips across his lap. Despite kissing him, she was sobbing. He made a shushing, soothing sound, a word that was not in the dictionary and could not be adequately transcribed. Its meaning, however, was clear, radiant, and long-lasting.

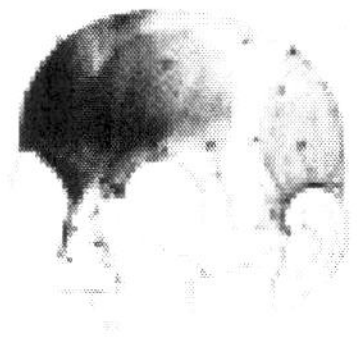

Sources

Allen, Gay Wilson, William James. New York: Viking Press, 1967.
Barzun, Jacques, A Stroll with William James. NY: Harper & Row, 1983.
Bittner, William, Poe, a Biography. London: Elek Books, 1963.
Cleator, P.E., Lost Languages. New York: John Day Co., 1959.
Draaisma, Douwe, Metaphors of Memory: A History of Ideas About the Mind. Cambridge: Cambridge University Press, 2000.
Hancocks, David, A Different Nature: The Paradoxical World of Zoos and Their Uncertain Future. Berkeley: U of Calif Press, 2001.
Inwood, Stephen, The Forgotten Genius: The Biography of Robert Hooke 1635-1703. San Francisco: MacAdam/Cage, 2003.
O'Donnell, John M., The Origins of Behaviorism: American Psychology, 1870-1920. New York: New York University Press, 1985.
Sigmund, Karl, Games of Life: Explorations in Ecology, Evolution and Behavior. London: Penguin Books, 1995.
Throckmorton, Peter, Diving for Treasure. New York: Viking, 1977.
Turner, Mark, The Literary Mind. Oxford: Oxford University Press, 1996.
Weyl, Hermann, Symmetry. Princeton: Princeton University Press, 1952.

ALSO AVAILABLE FROM RAVENNA PRESS

Mario Bellatin: *Chinese Checkers*
Daniel Borzutzky: *Arbitrary Tales*
Harold Bowes: *If Nothing Else*
Garth Buckner: *The Origins of Solitude*
John Burgess: *Punk Poems*
Robert Castle: *The End of Travel*
Gregory Cole: *The Moodier Could of Being*
Denis Emorine: *No Through World*
Cooper Esteban: *Mosefolket*
Soren Gauger: *Quatre Regards sur L'Enfant Jesus*
Brandon Hobson: *The Levitationist*
Lynn Kozlowski: *Historical Markers*
Barbara Kremen: *The Damsel Fly*
Frank Lentricchia: *The Book of Ruth*
Nathan Leslie: *Reverse Negative*
Oswald LeWinter: *Ages of Chaos and Fury*
Norman Lock: *The Long Rowing Unto Morning*
Norman Lock: *Notes to "The Book of Supplemental Diagrams" for Marco Knauff's Universe*
Norman Lock: *Trio*
Norman Lock: *Two Plays for Radio*
Rebecca Loudon: *Radish King*
Rebecca Loudon: *Tarantella*
Jody McAuliffe: *My Lovely Suicides*
Bryan McCarvey: *Temple Grounds*
Cathy Nilon: *Chemo Cat* (nonfiction)
Kathryn Rantala: *The Plant Waterer*
M Sarki: *Little War Machine*
Ron Starr: *A Map By a Dim Lamp*
John Sweet: *Human Cathedrals*
Daris Swindler: *New Britain Diary, 1954: An Anthropologist's Journal* (nonfiction)
Gene van Troyer (ed.): *Collaborations*
Faruk Ulay: *Terra Infirma*
Jane Unrue: *Atlassed*
Thomas Wooten: *In the Tabloid City*

UPCOMING TITLES

MTC Cronin: *Irrigations (of the Human Heart)*
James McCurry: *Indium*

Ravenna Press books are available at www.ravennapress.com and, via our Distributor, AtlasBooks, to individuals and the trade.